# Cassie's Cage Mystery

Advance Publishers, L.C.
1060 Maitland Center Commons, Suite 365
Maitland, FL 32751 USA

10 9 8 7 6 5 4 3 2 1
ISBN-10: 1-57973-393-X

It was Monday morning, and Handy Manny and the tools were talking about their plans for the coming week.

"I'm going to try not to break anything this week," Pat said. "That's my plan."

"That's not really a plan," Turner said.

"Well, I have a fabulous plan!" Felipe said eagerly. "Truly ¡fabuloso!"

"Is it dangerous?" Rusty asked nervously.

"I don't like to cut in," Dusty said, "but I think I hear the phone ringing."

*Manny and the tools built a cozy tank for Cassie's land turtle and her babies.*

## TURTLES

Look! This baby turtle has hatched from its egg. Before it hatched, its mommy dug a nest hole on land. She laid her eggs in the hole and covered them with dirt. The dirt keeps the eggs warm.

Cassie was calling from her pet store to ask Manny and the tools for help.

"Is there a *problema* with the turtle tank we built for you?" Manny asked.

Turtles carry their own shelters wherever they go!

## TURTLES

When a turtle feels afraid, it hides inside its shell. That's right! It just tucks its head, legs, and tail totally inside. It's like it's shutting the door to its house!

"Oh, no, there's no problem," Cassie said. "The turtle loves his tank! Today I need your help building a big new cage."

*Even Stretch isn't long enough to measure a giraffe!*

**GIRAFFES**
Giraffes are the tallest of all animals. Some can grow to be 20 feet tall. That's as tall as a house!

"What kind of cage does Cassie need?" Pat asked when Manny got off the phone.

"*No se*—I don't know," Manny said. "I forgot to ask her."

"She said a BIG cage, so maybe it's for a giraffe," Stretch said. "They're the tallest animals of all."

*If Cassie has a giraffe, she's going to need a very big water dish!*

## GIRAFFES

Giraffes live in the dry grasslands of Africa. It's not easy for giraffes to drink. They must spread their legs very wide. A giraffe can drink up to four gallons of water at a time.

On the way to Cassie's pet store, Manny and the tools saw Mr. Lopart.

"Do you need anything from the pet store, Mr. Lopart?" Manny asked.

### KITTENS
Look at all these tiny kittens! They are just a few days old. They cannot see or hear yet. They are sleeping. When they wake up, they will drink their mommy's milk.

"No, thank you," Mr. Lopart said, "I'm planning to go there myself to buy some cat toys. I'm just a little tied up at the moment."

*Do you know anyone who has a perro as a pet?*

## DOGS

The dog is often called man's best friend. That's because dogs are easy to train, and they make loyal companions.

Manny made a quick stop at the hardware store for hinges for the new cage.

"The fire department just got a dog from Cassie's Pet Store," Kelly told Manny. "They're going to train it to help them with their work."

"That must be a smart dog!" Squeeze said.
"*Si*," Manny said. "¡A very smart *perro!*"

*Snakes can be small or big, camouflaged or colorful.*

## SNAKES

Snakes can be found all over the world. They live in rain forests, woodlands, swamps, and deserts. Most snakes live in warm places.

"Cassie also has a new snake at her pet store," Kelly said. "I met it when I was there the other day."

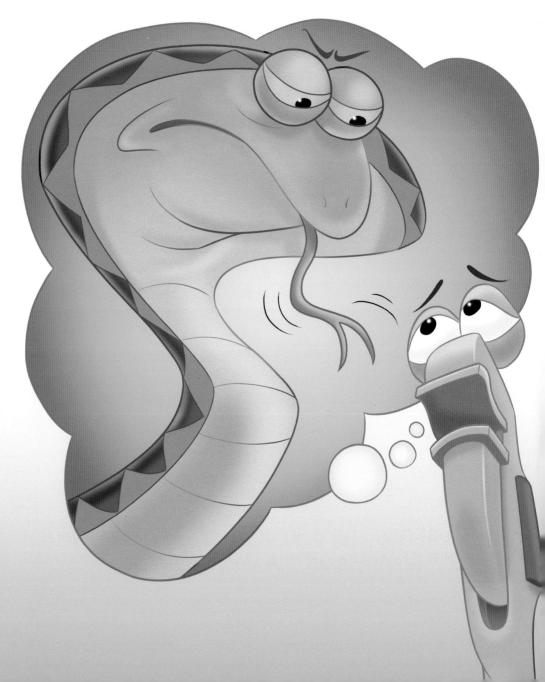

"Oh, no!" Rusty said. "I'm not so sure I want to meet a snake."

"Why not?" Pat asked. "Are you feeling shy?"

*Many snakes, including this ball python, are very shy.*

## BALL PYTHONS

Ball pythons have a shy and gentle nature. When they get nervous, ball pythons curl up into tight balls, hiding their heads inside.

**HUMMINGBIRDS**

Hummingbirds are the smallest birds in the world. The tiniest hummingbird, called the bee hummingbird, is only 2-1/2 inches long!

The tools loved to visit Cassie's pet store. There were always so many different kinds of animals to see. Today, they were especially eager to find out what kind of big new animal needed a big new cage.

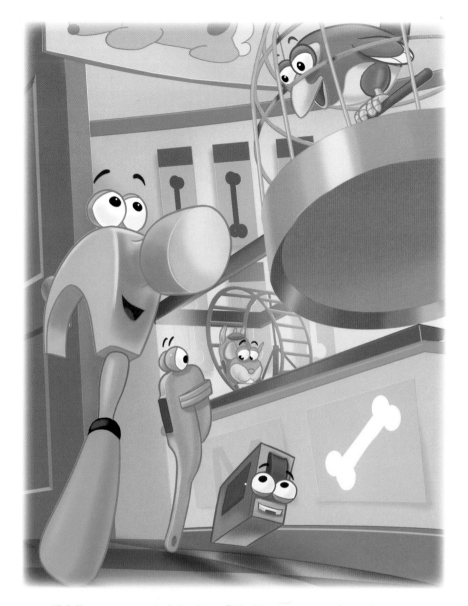

*Do you think Cassie has an ostrich at her pet store?*

## OSTRICHES
The ostrich is the largest bird in the world. Although it cannot fly, the ostrich can run about 40 miles per hour—faster than any other bird!

"What could it be?" Rusty asked nervously.

"It's a mystery!" Dusty said.

"Well, birds come in lots of different sizes," Stretch said. "Maybe Cassie needs a cage for a very large bird."

*As Cassie's snake grows, it will shed its skin and wear the new one underneath!*

## SNAKE SKIN

As snakes grow, their skin gets too small for their bodies. They wriggle around until the old skin comes off. Underneath, they have fresh new skin that's just the right size!

Just then Cassie came out to meet them with the new snake on her arm!

"A snake is a reptile," Cassie explained. "You can touch his scales if you want to."

"I'm feeling a little shy," Pat said.

"He's just a baby," Cassie said. "He's going to grow much bigger than this."

"Is that why you need a big new cage?" Turner asked.

*Have you seen rabbits near your home?*

**RABBITS**

Rabbits live in many places, from swamps and woodlands to tropical forests and deserts!

"The big new cage isn't for the snake," Manny said as Cassie hurried off to help a customer.

"Is it for a giraffe?" Stretch asked.

"No, it's not for a *jirafa*," Manny said.

"Is it for a very large bird?" Squeeze asked.

"It's not for a big *ave*, either," Manny laughed. "Cassie needs a bigger cage because one of the rabbits is going to have babies soon, and they won't all fit in the old cage.

## RABBITS

Rabbits usually live in groups in underground burrows. They eat grass, bark, leaves, and berries.

*Elephant herds need plenty of space to roam.*

## ELEPHANTS

There are many places in the world where elephants live. They stay together in a big group called a herd. Mothers, babies, grandmothers, aunts, cousins, brothers, and sisters all live together. They take care of one another.

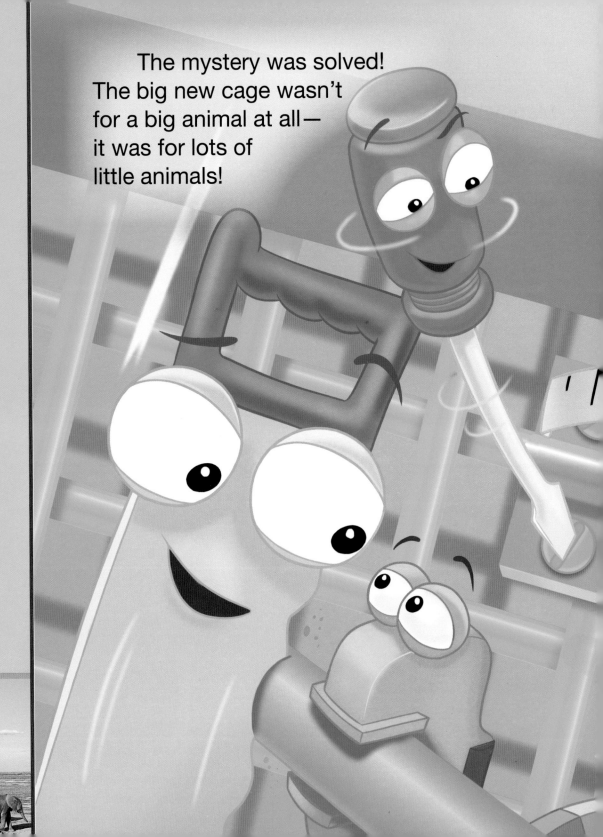

The mystery was solved! The big new cage wasn't for a big animal at all— it was for lots of little animals!

"We'll make the biggest and best baby bunny cage ever!" Dusty said as the tools all got to work.

"This cage will be big," Felipe said, "but it won't be the biggest ever. Someday I'm going to build something *grande* enough for a whole herd of elephants!"

*An elephant's trunk is almost as useful as one of Manny's tools!*

## ELEPHANTS

An elephant uses its trunk for breathing, smelling, and picking up favorite foods— such as hay, grasses, and plant roots— and putting them in its mouth. To clean off, elephants suck water into their trunks and then hose themselves down.

*The new rabbit kits will have a comfortable place to cuddle up.*

## KITS

This mommy rabbit has five new babies. Baby rabbits are called kits. Kits do not have fur when they are born. They snuggle close to one another to stay warm in their burrow.

Cassie was thrilled with the new rabbit cage! "This will be such a good home for the new kits," she said.

"Did you say kits?" Dusty asked. "I thought we were building the cage for baby bunnies."

Rabbit kits grow fast, so it's a good thing there's plenty of extra room in the new cage!

## KITS

Now look! The kits are two weeks old. They now have fur and are able to hop. Soon they will go off on their own. In three or four months they will have their own babies!

"Baby bunnies are called kits," Cassie explained.

"I never heard that before," Turner said suspiciously. "And I've been around for a while."

## SPANISH WORDS

**Fabuloso**
Fabulous

**Problema**
Problem

**No se**
I don't know

**Si**
Yes

**Perro**
Dog

**Jirafa**
Giraffe

**Ave**
Bird

**Grande**
Big

On the way home, the tools talked excitedly about the day.

"Can we go back when the rabbit kits are born?" Dusty asked.

"And to see how big the snake is getting…" Felipe said.

"And to visit the little birds!" Pat said.

"Sure!" Manny laughed.

"How about tomorrow?" asked Squeeze.